DARE
TO
DREAM

DARE TO DREAM

WAYNE B. LYNN

Bookcraft
Salt Lake City, Utah

Library of Congress Catalog Card Number: 92-70552
ISBN 0-88494-826-9

First Printing, 1992

Printed in the United States of America

You see things; and you say
    "why?"
But I dream things that never were;
    and I say, "why not?"

—George Bernard Shaw

Contents

Contents

Introduction:
Dare to Dream

To live life fully, we must dare to dream, to aspire. Dreams give life purpose, worth, enjoyment. They give us reason for living. Without them, much of life is wasted.

Theodore Roosevelt said: "Far better it is to dare mighty things, to win glorious triumphs, even though checkered by failure, than to take rank with those poor spirits who neither enjoy much nor suffer much, because they live in the gray twilight that knows not victory nor defeat."

In the first part of this book I have tried to give encouragement to carve and pursue dreams. In the second part I identify some of the obstacles we face, and suggest some ways to overcome them. And the final chapter is a reminder that life keeps going and growing—and so can our dreams.

Life offers us a blank check. The amount in reserve is unknown, but large. We decide how much to withdraw, and that determines what life will return to us. The tragedy of many people's lives lies in their gross underestimation of the size of the deposit in their account. Too frequently we imagine our reserve of talent and potential achievement to be nearly bankrupt. We even tend to defensively hoard that small amount against any imaginable setbacks.

Instead we should be deciding how best to invest our vast resources. We should turn our dreams and our resources into projects and processes which bring even greater worth to life.

This idea was expressed many years ago by Jessie B. Rittenhouse in a poem from *The Door of Dreams*:

My Wage

I bargained with Life for a penny,
    And Life would pay no more,
However I begged at evening
    When I counted my scanty store;

For Life is a just employer,
    He gives you what you ask,
But once you have set the wages,
    Why, you must bear the task.

I worked for a menial's hire,
    Only to learn, dismayed,
That any wage I had asked of Life,
    Life would have paid.

Part One

*You've Got
to Have
a Dream*

— 1 —

The Worth
of a Dream

There is an old saying, "If you don't know where you're going, any road will take you there." Unfortunately many people wander through life without knowing where they are going. But how can we get someplace, or at least know when we have arrived, if we don't know where we are going? It is right for us to make plans. It is right for us to have a destination. And it is right for us to dream, for our dreams help determine what our tomorrows will bring.

From his moving automobile Elder Thomas S. Monson observed a hitchhiker standing near the entrance to a freeway on-ramp, holding up a home-made sign that read simply, "Anywhere." Elder Monson commented, "Here was one who was content to travel in any direction, according to the whim of the driver who stopped to give him a free ride. What an enormous price to pay for such a ride. No plan. No objective. No goal. The road to anywhere is the road to nowhere, and the road to nowhere leads to dreams sacrificed, opportunities squandered, and a life unfulfilled." ("Which Road Will You Travel?" *Ensign*, November 1976, p.51.)

We need dreams. We can make them come true. What is a man without a dream? Dreams give purpose to our lives, a reason for living. There are big dreams and little dreams. There are dreams that are easily achieved and those that require us to climb to great heights as we seek to fulfill them. One poet said:

> I raised my eyes to yonder heights
> And longed for lifting wings
> To bear me to their sunlit crests
> As on my spirit sings.
> And though my feet must keep the paths
> That wind along the valley's floor,
> Yet after every upward glance
> I'm stronger than before.
>
> —Authorship unknown

Some dreams may require all our strength and resolve. Pursuing them will stretch us beyond what we consider to be our natural abilities and thus lift us to new levels of achievement. There are also shattered dreams which can break hearts and vanquish hope. These ruined dreams must be swept up, reexamined, pieced together so that we can start anew. But whatever our circumstances, we must have a dream, for a life is not whole without a dream.

Some dreams may be beyond reach. Perhaps we wonder what purpose is served by dreams unfulfilled or lofty plans not achieved. Are such dreams only a source of disappointment and frustration? Emphatically no! Such plans, though unattained or even futile, give purpose and direction to our lives for a time. Our worthy dreams move us forward and upward, and even the frustrations can help us properly adjust our goals and direction.

Some people dream of colonizing the moon. This dream is not yet realized. So the dream is useless, right? Wrong! I can name several benefits derived as a result of the pursuit. For instance, as I labor to write these words, I do so with relative ease by using my computer. The technology was first developed to lift men into space, then channeled into other applications such as word processing. When I fry an egg on our teflon frying pan and watch that egg slide smoothly from the pan, I often give silent thanks to those who dreamed of a perfect heat shield and designed nose cones which could withstand the great temperatures generated when a space vehicle reenters the earth's atmosphere.

Many people who dream of attaining a certain profession or occupation find themselves doing something different from what they had originally prepared to do. However, the pursuit of their original goal gave them experience, exposure to other alternatives, and the opportunity to grow toward wider possibilities. Knowledge gained in any vocational or academic training can often be applied in other fields and open doors that might otherwise be closed to us.

Those who have played defensive positions on a football team know how important it is to "stay alive" on their feet. It is much easier to move toward the correct defensive location when you are already in motion. Similarly, a tennis player moves his body from side to side, even though he is not yet certain which way he will have to go to return the ball. It is better for all of us to be moving, even if we have to change direction, than to be caught flat-footed, doing nothing. It is better to try, perhaps to fail and try again, than to sit idly by. Unobtained dreams are better than no dreams at all. We must dare to dream, for dreams give us purpose for living. In the musical play *South Pacific,* one of the characters observes that we need to have a dream; for without a dream, "how you gonna have a dream come true?"

The Man Who Thinks He Can

If you think you are beaten, you are;
    If you think you dare not, you don't.
If you like to win, but think you can't,
    It's almost a cinch you won't.
If you think you'll lose, you're lost,
    For out in the world we find
Success begins with a fellow's will;
    It's all in the state of mind.

If you think you are outclassed, you are;
    You've got to think high to rise.
You've got to be sure of yourself before
    You can ever win a prize.
Life's battles don't always go
    To the stronger or faster man;
But soon or late the man who wins
    Is the man who thinks he can.

                —Walter D. Wintle

— 2 —

Carve Your Own Dreams

On the front porch of the country store, a group of older men were sitting in the warmth of the afternoon sun. One man was slowly tipping back and forth in a rocking chair, idly watching his part of the world go by. A companion in conversation was seated next to him, a pile of wood shavings strewn carelessly at his feet and a sharpened pocketknife held firmly in his hand. "Just don't see how you can do that, Howard," the rocking companion mused. "That old piece of wood is now a horse, and I can even tell you whose horse it is."

"Nothin' to it," his companion retorted. "I just look at this piece of wood until I can see the horse inside it, and then I slice off the wood that's in the way."

This old sage was echoing the words of the great

r and artist Michelangelo, who, while peering at a large block of uncarved stone, said, "I will let Moses out."

When we see our dreams as clearly as Michelangelo saw the uncarved Moses, we can carve away the things that stand in the way until those dreams become a reality. By this process an architect's drawing becomes translated into a building. First comes the dream. Then he creates something to represent the dream, perhaps a full-color picture, complete with landscaping and minute detail. But the building hasn't yet been constructed. A housewife kneads a wad of sticky dough, while in her mind she imagines fragrant loaves of golden brown bread or a pan filled with mouth-watering cinnamon rolls. The master teacher sees more than an unkempt boy in ragged Levi's slouching in a chair. She visualizes a statesman, a scientist, an author. She sees her young charges not as they are, but as they may become. The Master Builder has told us: "For I, the Lord God, created all things, of which I have spoken, spiritually, before they were naturally upon the face of the earth" (Moses 3:5).

The following poem by William Croswell Doane expresses well the concepts discussed above:

Life Sculpture

Chisel in hand stood a sculptor boy
    With his marble block before him,
And his eyes lit up with a smile of joy,
    As an angel dream passed o'er him.

He carved the dream on that shapeless stone,
    With many a sharp incision;
With Heaven's own light the sculpture shown—
    He'd caught that angel vision.

Children of life are we, as we stand
  With our lives uncarved before us,
Waiting the hour when, at God's command,
  Our life dream shall pass o'er us.

If we carve it then on the yielding stone,
  With many a sharp incision,
Its heavenly beauty shall be our own,
  Our lives that angel vision.

The Lord has blessed us with wonderful minds that have the power of spiritual creativity. The designer sees a finished building in his mind before he puts the idea on paper, before the first spadeful of dirt is lifted. The gardener plows a new field, drops tiny seeds into the waiting soil, and nurtures the seeds into tender plants. His brow is covered with sweat as he toils to cultivate in the hot summer sun. He works willingly because of his vision of what these plants will become. He dreams of the joy that accompanies a rich and abundant harvest. One of life's greatest pleasures is to transform these mental pictures, these dreams, into reality.

Elder Sterling W. Sill shared these observations: "Shakespeare talked about the things that he could see in what he called his 'mind's eye.' When Wilbur Wright was eleven years old, he said to his father, 'Can a man fly?' Wilbur discussed this idea with his younger brother Orville. They would often sit up until long past midnight, fascinated by the fact that in their 'mind's eye' they could see themselves flying. Finally this great dream paid off, and they forever broke the shackles that for so long had bound man to earth." (*Church News*, March 5, 1966, p. 13.)

The countless hours the musician spends in practice are preceded by his dreams. Perhaps he visualizes performing beautiful music with such skill that it appears effortless. In like manner, the athlete envisions himself making that crucial score in front of a cheering crowd. A runner envisions breaking the tape at the finish line. It is his dream of success that carries him through the arduous labor and pain required to get him there. The dream sustains and drives him to forfeit easier or more pleasant pursuits because he knows that realizing the dream will be well worth the cost.

Peter Vidmar, world Olympic champion, said it this way: "But there is one quality that rises above all, and without it, the athlete is not complete. That ingredient is desire. . . . Just imagine what it's like to be an Olympic champion! Imagine the feeling of having that medal placed around your neck as you stand on the victory platform." ("Pursuing Excellence," *Ensign,* May 1985, pp. 38, 40.) To reach his goal, Peter trained as much as six hours a day, six days a week, investing, it seemed, all of his energy and resources. But . . . his dream came true. He carved his own dream. The poet said:

> Dream, oh youth; dream nobly and manfully,
> And thy dreams shall be thy prophets.
>
> —Authorship unknown

General H. Norman Schwarzkopf commanded the vast military might of the Coalition to Free Kuwait. Here was the fulfillment of a dream of a boy being prepared to serve his country. *Time* magazine reported that "when photos were taken for the yearbook at Bordertown Military Institute, near Trenton, ten-year-old cadet Norman posed for two pictures, one smiling, the other grim-faced. His mother preferred the smiling version, but little Norman hung tough. 'Someday,' he explained, 'when I become a general, I want people to know that I'm serious.' He wasn't kidding." (*Time,* February 4, 1991, p. 30.)

Dreams can come true because we can *make* them come true. We can carve our dreams out of the brittle stone of adversity and the softer wood of everyday living. We can then take a step back to admire the work and to thrill in the joy of our creation. With the help of the Lord, we have made our dream a beautiful reality. Hold fast to your dreams.

Hold Fast Your Dreams

Hold fast your dreams!
Within your heart
Keep one still, secret spot
Where dreams may go,
And, sheltered so,
May thrive and grow
Where doubt and fear are not.
O keep a place apart,
Within your heart,
For little dreams to go!

Think still of lovely things that are not true.
Let wish and magic work at will in you.
Be sometimes blind to sorrow. Make believe!
Forget the calm that lies
In disillusioned eyes.
Though we all know that we must die,
Yet you and I
May walk like gods and be
Even now at home in immortality.

We see so many ugly things—
Deceits and wrongs and quarrelings;
We know, alas! we know
How quickly fade

Dare to Dream

The color in the west,
The bloom upon the flower
The bloom upon the breast
And youth's blind hour.
Yet keep within your heart
A place apart
Where little dreams may go,
May thrive and grow.
Hold fast—hold fast your dreams!

—Louise Driscoll

— 3 —

First
Begin

B egin. The rest will follow. Have you ever
watched would-be swimmers on the bank
of a cold mountain stream? The longer they stand on
the bank and contemplate the icy plunge, the more
difficult the venture becomes. This is like many ven-
tures in life. The importance of just beginning was eloquently expressed in a couplet attributed to Goethe:

> Whatever you can do, or dream you can, begin it.
> Boldness has genius, power and magic in it.

As a former shop teacher and a somewhat left-
handed carpenter, I have learned from experience the
value of beginning. Even a false start is a start, and it
will lead to ultimate progress. In carpentry, problems

of design or structure that seemed nearly insoluble before beginning become solvable as small discoveries come with the doing. Inspiration incubates in a climate of activity and creativity. One idea gives birth to another, and you are able to complete what you began.

Once one is committed to a course of action, things begin to happen that lead to success. The important thing is to begin, and to begin with commitment.

While teaching shop in high school I noted that my most successful students were those who had no fear of making mistakes. They learned that it is no disgrace to not know how to do something. Regrets came instead when they were so concerned about showing their inexperience that they forfeited an opportunity to grow or to learn. With some it appears that the fear of failure is greater than the desire to succeed.

This same principle applies in nearly every facet of life. If we view challenges as exciting adventures into the unknown rather than as forbidding obstacles, our lives can take on exciting new dimensions. Perhaps that is why youngsters adapt so readily to computers. They have no fear of failure or of trying something new. Consequently they often leave their more timid elders behind.

Take courage to begin. What have you got to lose?

I recall a time when my students competed with students from other schools to demonstrate skills acquired in their shop training. One of my regular team members failed to appear, leaving us one man short. I was anxious to find an instant replacement to meet the number required for team competition. A freshman was working nearby on some construction. I had previously noted his willingness to tackle any kind of project. Not by inspiration but out of desperation, I enlisted him for my team and gave him a thirty-minute crash course on how to weld with an oxyacetylene welding torch. To say that he was ill-prepared is an understatement.

Soon we were off to the neighboring town, experiencing the thrill of competition. My little freshman was thrown to the wolves. It was like suiting him up in a football uniform for the first time and then sending him into the thick of a varsity ball game. There was a dramatic contrast between the metal pieces he welded and the ones welded by the senior boy who won the contest. The piece so skillfully welded by the winner was nearly a piece of art. The weld was smooth and strong. It penetrated the metal as a good weld should. He had clearly mastered this useful skill.

My freshman was undaunted, however, by what could have been an embarrassing situation. I watched him congratulate the winner and heard him make a rather startling request: "Can I have your welded piece to take home with me?"

Puzzled by the request, the winner replied, "Of course you can."

It was particularly satisfying for me to watch that boy in the days that followed. Each shop period I watched him working in the corner of the shop where the welders were kept. Wearing goggles and protective gloves, he worked under rising smoke, practicing his welding skills. Next to his own work he always placed the prize-winning weld of his former competitor. When it wasn't out for observation, it was always in his shop coverall pocket. He was determined to make a weld to match that one. His efforts were sustained by such a stubborn determination that it became a joke among some of the other students. Following each shop class he would have a circle around each eye, battle marks from the welder's goggles held tightly around his head by an elastic band.

In the beginning his welds were crude. Instruction,

observation, and encouragement helped, but improvement came primarily from his constant practice and determination. You can guess the outcome of this story. One day I thrilled to watch him walk across the stage of a packed auditorium to receive recognition for outstanding acetylene welding in state competition. He not only matched the weld in his pocket, he made a better one. He was not afraid to try. By applying this kind of determination to other goals in his life, he went on to other achievements.

The secret is to begin. It is never too late to try new challenges or establish new goals. Elder Richard L. Evans said, "The tragedy of life is not that it ends so soon, but that we wait so long to begin it."

Mountains viewed from a distance often appear impossible to ascend. But mountaintops are reached by those who are not afraid to begin the climb. They begin with easy steps up gentle foothills which lead to steeper slopes. They are not intimidated by sheer cliffs; instead they move close enough to see the hidden clefts. They find footholds on slopes that initially appeared to be vertical angles. There will be surprises too. Some obstacles will be more difficult than supposed, but each new experience will provide an increased ability to achieve. Some cliffs will need to be circumvented, but the climb is ever upward until we breathe the sweet air at the crest of the mountain.

We must not put off our efforts by saying, "When I get older," or, "If I were only younger." Thomas Jefferson was thirty-three years old when he drafted the Declaration of Independence. Charles Dickens was twenty-five when he wrote *Oliver Twist* and only twenty-four when he penned the *Pickwick Papers*. Joseph Smith was twenty-three when he translated the Book of Mormon and twenty-four when he was directed to organize The Church of Jesus Christ of

Latter-day Saints. On the other hand, Alfred Lord Tennyson was eighty years old when he wrote "Crossing the Bar," and Titian may have been in his nineties when he began painting his later version of *Christ Crowned with Thorns.*

To truly succeed in life, whatever our age, we need to climb life's mountains, in whatever form they come. Watching mountain climbers on TV will not strengthen our leg muscles or enlarge our lung capacity. Eleanor Roosevelt said it this way: "I could not at any age be content to take my place in a corner by the fireside and simply look on. Life was meant to be lived. One must never, for whatever reason, turn his back on life." Consider these lines from a famous play:

> There is a tide in the affairs of men,
> Which, taken at the flood, leads on to fortune;
> Omitted, all the voyage of their life
> Is bound in shallows and in miseries. . . .
> And we must take the current when it serves,
> Or lose our ventures.
>
> —William Shakespeare, *Julius Caesar*

— 4 —

You Can Do It!

I would like to talk to you confidentially for a few minutes, President." So began many conversations when I was a mission president.

"Of course, come on into my office. What's on your mind?"

The visitors were older couples anxious to share a concern. "President, we are anxious to serve, but we feel you ought to know that we can never proselyte." Or, "I haven't always been very active in the Church, so please don't ask me to preside." Or, "Don't ask me to conduct music or teach a class." I could continue, but I think you get the drift.

I must have caused these missionaries some uneasiness when I appeared to not be listening very closely. The truth is, I wasn't. I recognized a pattern, and experience had demonstrated to me that they could achieve much more than they thought possible, regardless of lack of previous experience or of perceived limitations. In short, I had more confidence in them than they frequently had in themselves. I came to agree with Lamoni's words to Ammon, "I know, in the strength of the Lord thou canst do all things" (Alma 20:4).

As challenges came and the couples, out of necessity, rose to meet them, they often discovered talents and abilities that had lain dormant for years. They developed skills and accomplished things they had not thought possible. It was Robert Browning who said:

> Ah, but a man's reach should
>   exceed his grasp,
> Or what's a heaven for?

Let me share a dramatic illustration. One couple arrived in the mission frightened beyond reason of what they thought would be expected of them. Their experience before their mission call was limited to the area where they lived. During the excellent training offered at the Missionary Training Center, they were in company with other couples assigned to our mission. This gave them some comfort and assurance. When they reached the mission home, however, the prospect of serving alone in an area of assignment was almost overwhelming. What added more to their fears was the fact that much of our mission was in Indian territory. "The only Indians we've ever seen were in the movies—and they were on the warpath," they said.

Trying to bolster them, I assigned two of my young Navajo elders to accompany them to their assigned area of the reservation. These young Navajos were fine, educated, spiritual young men serving full-time missions. They were handsome and well-groomed in their dark suits, white shirts, and ties. They were a credit both to the Church and to their people. However, I learned later that even the experience of being alone with these two Indians for the afternoon nearly frightened the couple to death.

It was almost dark that evening when the couple returned from the reservation. Obviously shaken, they came into my office. The sister was crying quietly. She took a seat toward the back corner of my office. Her husband was spokesman for both of them.

"President, the worst place in the world that I know is our state penitentiary, but I would rather spend the next year there than go where you want to assign us out on that reservation."

I was a bit surprised at this declaration since the living quarters there were better than most, and the location was in a relatively accessible area. I reassured him by saying, "First, let me put you at ease. I promise not to send you anywhere you don't want to go. If we can't find a place in this mission, then we'll find one for you in another."

I then picked up a map that I had pasted on heavy posterboard. "See these yellow tacks?" I asked him. "Each of these represents a place where I need couples to assist us. Why don't you both look this map over and see if you can find a place where you feel you might want to serve. Pray about it. Tomorrow morning we'll see how things work out." We separated for the evening.

They prayed in faith, and then chose a potential area of assignment. After a good night's sleep and a hearty breakfast, the couple returned to my office. They announced their decision and pointed out the area where they felt impressed to serve. We gave them directions to follow and waved good-bye. With some trepidation they started on their way. Through faith they were able to take a courageous step into the unknown. Fortunately the Lord had helped guide them to an area where two fine young elders were serving nearby.

Three weeks later I was in that area to conduct a mission zone conference to which they had been invited. The conference began as usual with my conducting personal interviews with each missionary. On this particular morning I started interviewing at daylight. Late in the morning, I saw this good brother coming toward me for an interview. His countenance was far different from the one I had last observed. When he saw me, his pace quickened and a smile came to his face. I didn't have to prompt him to tell me how things were going.

"Those young elders serving with us are the finest young men on the face of the earth," was his opening comment. Then he said, "I always thought the people where we came from were the friendliest people anywhere; but, President, these Navajo Indians . . . "

He paused, with a catch in his voice. His handkerchief was out and he was wiping his eyes. He smiled with embarrassment, and then, in halting words, he described his departure that morning as he left his home to attend the conference. "One little feller followed me out to the car. When he could see that I was leaving, he wrapped himself around my leg and held on." He dragged his foot stiffly to demonstrate how he had tried to progress to his car. "I finally picked him up," he said, "and he planted a kiss right here." Pointing to a spot on the side of his face he continued. "He had been eating candy and his face was sticky. His mouth stuck to my cheek so that he could hardly let go."

By this time the tears were flowing again, reaching

the upturned corners of his mouth. Needless to say I quit worrying about how this good brother and his wife were going to get along with the Indians.

This was a starting point for this couple. When they left the area some months later, it was with tender tears and declarations of love. Many of the Indian people who had reached out to help them were themselves blessed. The world was a better place because this couple had been there.

This is only one of many stories that could be told. Over and over I saw missionaries take a step into the unknown and emerge stronger, brighter, more capable than they themselves ever dreamed possible. Young missionaries who had barely passed ninth-grade arithmetic classes discovered they could keep books for a very complex financial operation that included the rent and maintenance of many housing units, vehicles, operation expenses, rental agreements, vehicle titles and licensing. These tasks were given to nineteen-year-olds whose mothers knew that the young men couldn't previously balance a checkbook. Yet they grew into the job and thrived on the challenge.

Of course they could do it! And just as surely, you can do what you need to do! You don't have to be young. You don't have to be old. You don't have to be a missionary. Just don't be afraid to try.

— 5 —

Dreams Have a Price

Great things happen when people dare to dream, but dreams remain unsubstantial unless something is done to make them happen. Things of value have a price attached and we must pay the price. In reaching back for an example to illustrate this principle, I recall a certain basketball team.

The shouting had subsided. The game was over. Emotionally spent, and with their ears still ringing and voices grown hoarse with shouting, the spectators quietly waited in the gym. The announcer's amplified voice awakened the crowd from its respite. The noise and excitement swelled again as teams and individual players were introduced and trophies were awarded in recognition of outstanding performance. Flashbulbs popped, and sustained applause filled the air.

When the ceremonies ended, the coach and his players entered several waiting cars for the trip home.

They traveled through the darkness in silence. Busy with their own private thoughts, each was silently reliving random moments from the whirlwind of events just past. Snowflakes were landing softly on the windshield of the coach's car and the regular beat of the windshield wipers cast a hypnotic spell. Headlights strained against the enveloping darkness, lighting their progress down the highway.

Finally, tentatively, one young man who had been particularly honored that night spoke softly. "Coach," he said, "I think we were *supposed* to win tonight."

Silence again, except for the swish of tires through soft snow and the muffled sound of the engine. Then the coach, trying hard to contain his pent-up emotions, asked with a husky voice, "Why? Why do you think we were supposed to win?"

The response was simple and direct. "Because we paid the price."

What a great lesson for a young man to have learned and for a teacher to have taught! Winning the game took more than clever strategies and techniques. They had paid the full price in the day-to-day discipline of physical conditioning, teamwork, and a strong defense. This precious pearl of wisdom would serve these young men for a lifetime. Success happened because "we paid the price."

To appreciate the significance of the team's achievement, we need to know some of its history. A young man recently graduated from college accepted his first teaching assignment in a strange town in Wyoming, many miles from his native Utah. Dean L. Larsen (now Elder Dean L. Larsen of the Presidency of the Seventy) was hired not as a coach but as an English and Spanish teacher.

Through a chain of unforeseen events the school found itself approaching the basketball season without a coach. In that community the gravity of such a situation was like the plight of passengers in an airplane without a pilot. Young Mr. Larsen was invited to fill the critical vacancy. At least he could draw upon his experience in high school and college as an excellent athletic competitor.

Assuming such a responsibility on such short notice at the commencement of the season would have been a challenge for even the most experienced coach. But the task was made more difficult because Coach Larsen's system varied significantly from the style the boys were accustomed to. He relied on a fast break with quickly developing plays. This was an especially difficult adjustment for two of the taller senior boys, six foot six and six foot seven, respectively. Frequently the plays were completed before they could run to the other end of the floor. Therefore, they found their positions being threatened by some of the smaller, faster, more agile underclassmen. Their frustration soon developed into outright dissatisfaction.

The seriousness of the situation became apparent after the disastrous first game of the season. The team was soundly beaten by a team from a smaller school. The reaction was immediate! The whole town was upset! Basketball was more than just a game in Lovell, Wyoming; it was a matter of pride and personal honor.

By the time the team had experienced eight consecutive losses, the emotional climate surrounding the school and community was highly charged. Some townspeople no longer wondered *if* they should replace the coach but *how*. There was nothing personal in this determination. The coach's removal was seen as the solution to the town's and the team's failure. The two senior players quit, having lost sight of their dream of a successful season. The matter of how to get rid of the coach now became a subject for open discussion.

In spite of the negative fervor of some townspeople, the new coach was sustained by the school board of education. They decided to give him a chance and voted to retain him in the coaching position. The townspeople then more or less resigned themselves to a poor season.

The remaining players, however, were fiercely loyal to the coach. They had found a dream. They had faith in themselves and in their coach. They were confident of their ability to win and were willing to work for it. By midseason, however, they had won only one game out of nine and were resting firmly in eighth place in the conference standings. But though they were losing, they were playing hard and holding fast to the dream of winning.

In midseason the team did begin to win and, to the amazement of all, they finished third place in the conference tournament. Thus, by a narrow margin, they qualified for the state playoffs. Of course, by finishing so low in the qualifying tournament, they drew the toughest teams in the state for tournament competition.

By this time their strict discipline had paid off in excellent physical condition and a spirit of camaraderie, teamwork, and determination. The first game of the state finals was held in Powell, Wyoming, where the host school was proudly displaying their new gymnasium. The opening game of the tournament pitted Lovell against Lusk, the champions of the southeast district. The score was tied twelve times during the fierce battle—four times in the first quarter, four times in the second, and four times in the final period. One Lovell player had a "hot hand" and poured in sixteen points which kept the Bulldogs in the game. Lusk held a five-point halftime lead, but with six minutes to go Lovell tied the score. Thereafter Lusk led briefly, by one point, but Lovell spurted ahead to win by an eight-point margin!

Termed the "Cinderella Team of Wyoming" after this first victory, Lovell advanced to the semi-finals. With this momentum, they faced the ominous Reliance team, and to the delight of thousands of fans, trounced them by a score of 70 to 50.

For the championship game, carloads of fans drove bumper to bumper through near-blizzard conditions. The gymnasium filled to overflowing. Tension was high as the Lovell Bulldogs faced the awesome Worland Warriors for the final game. The Warriors had beaten the Bulldogs soundly in their last three encounters. The Bulldogs were clearly underdogs.

Fired with hope, the crowd cheered Lovell's Cinderella team as they took command early in the game. They jumped to a 23 to 11 first-quarter lead, and held the lead at halftime, 53 to 44. Without faltering, they outclassed and outplayed Worland. Final score: 70 to 65.

For the first time in the history of the school, this small town was the Wyoming State Champion! Headlines in the newspaper read: "Coach Larsen's Bulldogs Win 'Class A' Title." Subtitles read: "Coach Makes Most Startling Record in History of High School Basketball"; "Team Whips into Shape Late in Season to Place Third in Sub-State Meet"; "Finals at State Tourney Leave No Question About Superior Morale, Condition and Ability of Lovell Boys."

In the days that followed, the team and coach became a focal point. Dinners were held in their honor. Newspapers from all over the state carried stories of the rags-to-riches season. Coach Larsen was selected by the sportswriters of Wyoming as "Coach of the Year" and was given a beautifully engraved wrist-watch which he wears to this day.

Typical of the news articles is one extracted from the *Northern Wyoming Daily News*, whose headline read, "Laramie Paper Picks Lovell Mentor as Coach of Year":

> Youthful Dean Larsen, 25, who molded unranked and lightly regarded Lovell into state basketball champs his first time out following four previous Bulldog tourney failures, was saluted Thursday by the Laramie Daily Bulletin as the state's high school age Coach of the Year.
>
> It was Larsen, serving his freshman coaching stint at Lovell this term, by a landslide for the honor. No other mentor even figured in the Bulletin's selection. So astounding was Lovell's success at the single A state tournament at Powell that it must rank as the biggest surprise in schooolboy circles.

The players and their coach had a dream of winning. It came true through teamwork, conditioning, faith in their coach, and support from their fans. But the primary reason for the team's success was summed up in the quiet words of one of the players: "I believe we deserved to win, Coach. We paid the price."

Success

If you want a thing bad enough
 To go out and fight for it,
 Work day and night for it,
 Give up your time and your peace and your
  sleep for it,

Dreams Have A Price

If only a desire of it
Makes you quite mad enough
Never to tire of it,
Makes you hold all other things tawdry and
    cheap for it,
If life seems empty and useless without it
And all that you scheme and you dream is
    about it, . . .
If you'll simply go after that thing that you want,
With all your capacity,
Strength and sagacity,
Faith, hope and confidence, stern pertinacity,
If neither cold poverty, famished and gaunt,
Nor sickness nor pain,
Of body or brain
Can turn you away from the thing that you want,
If dogged and grim you besiege and beset it,
You'll get it!

                —Berton Braley

— 6 —

Choose Your Ruts Carefully

In rural Wyoming where I spent my youth, it was not uncommon to encounter long, dusty country roads. When we reached the end of a paved highway we were very cautious about our choice of roads from that point on. Our choices were often limited to dirt roads that were deeply grooved from the countless wheels that had passed over them. During the wet seasons of fall and winter these dirt roads became muddy and sometimes treacherous. Churning wheels dug deeply for traction, leaving behind long deep scars. Once having entered such a road, the traveler was committed to follow it; turning around was difficult, if not impossible. We often said to one another, "Choose your ruts carefully."

The same precaution could be applied to our lives.

The paths we choose become deeper with the passing of time. We form habits that are not easily broken. Changing direction is difficult. How much better it would be to form good habits from the beginning so that turning around is not necessary.

We are not born with habits. They develop as a result of our choices, both large and small. In the beginning we control our habits. By choosing to do something the same way over and over again, we develop habits. As life continues, our habits grow in strength, and they can begin to control us. We may become slaves to our own past performance. When we form good habits, they can be our best friends. Bad habits can become our worst enemies.

There are many good habits that can serve us well, such as the habit of being friendly or of looking on the brighter side of things. On the other hand, negative attitudes can be soul-destructive. It is our choice. Which habits do we want?

"Don't expect George yet. He is always late." Have you ever heard such expressions? Search your memory. Do you know someone who is always late? Perhaps a better question is, Who can you always count on to be on time? Isn't it interesting that when we adjust our clocks from daylight savings time and gain an hour, the people who were late before are still late? Change the meeting schedule to a later hour, and they are still tardy. Habit. Where do you fit in? Why not choose to be punctual? This would be a healthy habit for anyone to foster. The choice is yours.

Dependability is another habit to be desired. Correctly formed habits of being trustworthy and dependable will make life more pleasant for all and will help make your dreams come true.

Habits of praying daily, of observing the Sabbath, of reading scripture, and of accepting Church assignments and responsibilities will bring down the blessings of heaven and make your life happier.

The way we use our time is a habit that governs our lives. Do we stay up late, and then sleep in the next morning? Isn't this like cutting one end off a blanket and sewing it onto the other end to make it longer? Do we plan and use our spare time effectively? Have you ever noticed that when we are the busiest we seem to get the most accomplished? "Do not squander time, for that's the stuff life is made of" (Benjamin Franklin, *Poor Richard's Almanack,* June 1746).

Have you ever wondered how you would react in a time of crisis? Would I have chosen to cross the plains with the Saints? Would I react bravely in a situation that called for courage? Would I be a Laman or Lemuel in the wilderness, or would I be a Nephi or Sam? I would like to consider some of these questions by relating a personal experience.

A few years ago in Idaho a leak developed in the Teton Dam, causing the dam to give way suddenly and release millions of gallons of water. The torrent indiscriminately carried houses and cows, tractors and trailers, trees and shrubs in its ruinous path. Homes that weren't carried away were sometimes filled with dirty water and silt-laden sludge. It was a sobering event.

Afterward some of us who lived in neighboring areas were given the opportunity to assist the victims of this destruction. At 3:00 one morning my wife and I, along with many others, boarded a rented school bus to travel to the Rexburg area. When we were delayed at a roadblock, I received one of the great thrills of my life as I observed a line of buses, similarly loaded with volunteers, stretching as far as I could see in each direction down the highway. All were there to lend assistance.

We had a strenuous but joyous day in helping to clean, sort, and restore. During the day I talked with a bishop who was helping to direct our rescue efforts.

"Bishop," I said, "I would be interested to know how your people responded during this period of stress. Were there any surprises? Who did you find you could really count on?"

I was not surprised by his response. "As you know," he told me, "whenever you have a ward project or activity and call upon the members for assistance, you can pretty well predict who will be there and how much they will help. In this instance, I found that the predictable stalwarts who gave a helping hand in times past were the ones who came through for us this time."

How would we react if we were called to cross the plains in a covered wagon or handcart or to show courage in the face of danger? We would likely react in pretty much the same way we meet the many small but important situations we encounter from day to day. Each day we are becoming what we are to become.

Our habits reflect our innermost thoughts and character. How much, then, we should desire to develop good habits that will help us through life. It has been said, "Bad habits are like a comfortable bed—easy to get into, but hard to get out of." Make right choices because, as a philosopher stated, "the chains of habit are generally too small to be felt until they are too strong to be broken."

— 7 —

Setbacks as Stepping-Stones

No matter how carefully we plan our lives, and no matter how hard we try or how well we live, sooner or later we will all come face to face with adversity and failure. Someone truthfully stated, "Adversity has a date with every man. He may forget it, but she never does." Adversity may have a date with us, but as far as most of us are concerned it is a blind date.

If this date is to come, how can we prepare for it? Is this date with destiny only to be endured and then forgotten, or can it be more than that? While it would be imprudent for us to seek out this companion, this obstacle which seems to stand in the way of our growth and development can actually be used as a stepping-stone to new heights of achievement.

In all walks of life we find people who recognize that learning from their failures is one of the greatest contributions to their success. At the time of their failures they were undoubtedly discouraged, perhaps even self-doubting or despondent; yet as they applied their failure experiences to new efforts, their failures became stepping-stones. The scientist, the inventor, the composer may try something ten times, one hundred times, or even ten thousand times, and fail. But if he successfully applies the knowledge he has gained to the ten-thousand-and-first try, he is no longer a failure. He has succeeded.

One of the most important lessons we can learn from failures is that the human spirit is often strengthened by confronting disaster. When we face reverses in health or financial reserves, personal tragedies, or other problems, we can re-examine our dreams. Circumstances can force us to re-evaluate and modify our priorities. We may find that some of our dreams are not as important as we once thought them to be. This refining process can help create new dreams and give added meaning and direction to our lives. While we experience these problems we likely wish we didn't have them. However given the objectivity that comes with time, we may later conclude that our problems have become stepping-stones, lifting us toward the realization of even greater dreams.

This principle was beautifully expressed by Elder James E. Faust:

In the pain, the agony, and the heroic endeavors of life, we pass through a refiner's fire, and the insignificant and the unimportant in our lives can melt away like dross and make our faith bright, intact, and strong. In this way the divine image can be mirrored from the soul. It is part of the purging toll exacted of some to become acquainted with God. In the agonies of life, we seem to listen better to the faint, godly whisperings of the Divine Shepherd.

Into every life there come the painful, despairing days of adversity and buffeting. There seems to be a full measure of anguish, sorrow, and often heartbreak for everyone, including those who earnestly seek to do right and be faithful. The thorns that prick, that stick in the flesh, that hurt, often change lives which seem robbed of significance and hope. This change comes about through a refining process which often seems cruel and hard. In this way the soul can become like soft clay in the hands of the Master in building lives of faith, usefulness, beauty, and strength. For some, the refiner's fire causes a loss of belief and faith in God, but those with eternal perspective understand that such refining is part of the perfection process. ("The Refiner's Fire," *Ensign*, May 1979, p. 53.)

Elder Marion G. Romney said this: "I have seen the remorse and despair in the lives of men who, in the hour of trial, have cursed God and died spiritually. And I have seen people rise to great heights from what seemed to be unbearable burdens. Finally, I have sought the Lord in my own extremities and learned for myself that my soul has made its greatest growth as I have been driven to my knees by adversity and affliction." ("The Crucible of Adversity and Affliction," *Improvement Era,* October 1969, p. 69.)

To develop properly our bodies and our spirits must experience opposition. Mountain climbers develop leg muscles and strong lungs as they overcome the force of gravity and meet the challenges of the climb. Athletes train by using different forms of resistance to strengthen their muscles. Teachers offer students progressively difficult assignments and problems to solve so that they will strengthen their intellect and skills.

Athletic teams are never certain how good they are until they have been tested against strong competition and they have been required to give their best. We may learn little when the ground is smooth and requires little effort. Robert Browning Hamilton wrote:

Along the Road

I walked a mile with Pleasure;
    She chattered all the way,
But left me none the wiser
    For all she had to say.

I walked a mile with Sorrow
    And ne'er a word said she;
But oh, the things I learned from her
    When Sorrow walked with me!

Following this thought further, I quote from Henry Ward Beecher: "Affliction comes to us all, not to make us sad, but sober; not to make us sorry, but to make us wise; not to make us despondent, but by its darkness to refresh us as the night refreshes the day; not to impoverish, but to enrich us."

If we are shortsighted when we consider the effects of adversity, we may fail to see the refining and purifying effects that the flames of adversity bring.

My close friend had to endure excruciating pain with a failing heart. Physicians were eventually able to surgically repair the heart. What they were not able to do, and what my friend's repeated prayers did not accomplish, was to spare him from a great deal of intense pain. He told me, "I learned that the Lord does not always spare us from pain or suffering. What he did do for me was to give me the strength to endure it."

This was a principle I found I needed to teach over and over again when I presided over young missionaries. Some expected that they would experience little or no adversity while serving the Lord full-time. Such is not the case. There might even be more. Because the Lord loves us, he blesses us with challenges and obstacles, the overcoming of which strengthens our spiritual muscles. We will gain a life of happiness if, with the help of the Lord, we learn to cope with whatever circumstances come our way.

Elder Orson F. Whitney said: "No pain that we suffer, no trial that we experience is wasted. It ministers to our education, to the development of such qualities as patience, faith, fortitude and humility. All that we suffer . . . builds up our characters, purifies our hearts, expands our souls, and makes us more tender and charitable, more worthy to be called the children of God . . . and it is through sorrow and suffering, toil and tribulation, that we gain the education . . . which will make us more like our Father and Mother in heaven." (Cited in Spencer W. Kimball, *Faith Precedes the Miracle* [Salt Lake City: Deseret Book Co., 1972], p. 98.)

Let us take the pieces of our broken dreams, then, set them as stepping-stones, and use them to climb higher and reach even better dreams.

—WHAT ARE MY DREAMS?

—"WATCH FOR STEPPING STONES"—

Part Two

Making Our Dreams Come True

— 8 —

The Destroyer
of Dreams

During the many years when I worked in classrooms and rubbed shoulders with youth in the huge arena we call life, I learned about an enemy that vanquishes hope and shatters dreams. I call this ruthless foe "The Destroyer of Dreams." He is frightening, but he is a coward. Again and again I watched him try to thwart ambition and stifle achievement.

Behind the bravado of a super athlete or the facade of a bully, he hides and whispers, "You're not really so tough." Sometimes he lurks beside the shy student, twisting his thoughts so he'll believe he's not even worth notice. At other times he lies in wait, hoping to turn a cheerful smile or an exuberant personality into a mere mask. This Destroyer of Dreams is no respecter of persons. He does not discriminate by age, race, or social position. He seeks any vulnerable victim.

Dead at the feet of this Destroyer are piles of shattered dreams. Many were stillborn. Others lived a short time, only to be killed in infancy, never to mature and bring the sweetness of fulfillment.

Who is this ugly monster I have described? Perhaps you have failed to recognize him in the shadows where he hides. He is the demon who mimics our own voices, persuading a person that "I cannot achieve as others do." He is the enemy to accomplishment.

"I never could do math" is one of his favorite cliches. "I don't have the talent for that" is another of his well-worn tools. Legions of individuals frankly admit in moments of candor that they consider themselves to be not as smart or as talented or as gifted as others. They have adopted adaptive behaviors, but beneath the surface spreads a destructive virus. By his lies and exaggerations, the Destroyer of Dreams diminishes a person's sense of capability, poisoning the soul's lifeblood. Dreams remain undreamed, unrealized, and lifeless at the feet of the Destroyer.

"I'm not coordinated." "I have two left feet." "That takes money." "I came from a poor neighborhood." "Things never come easy for me." All of these expressions cause the Destroyer of Dreams to smile wickedly and rub his hands together in gleeful satisfaction. "As long as they think they can't . . . they can't! As long as they don't try . . . they won't accomplish anything. And I . . . I will remain the Destroyer!"

James Russell Lowell penned these words:

> Greatly begin! though thou have time
> But for a line, be that sublime.
> Not failure, but low aim, is crime.

42

This is the great disaster. Wasted human resources lie stagnant in the pool of unused potential of what might have been. Fear of failure makes us victim to the Destroyer who tries to convince us that, "You can't achieve as others do." A great educator who had spent years working with persons who were blind, deaf, or otherwise physically handicapped, said, "I have worked with many people who were more handicapped by their lack of self-confidence than by their physical disabilities."

In the following chapters I have tried to expose some of the methods used by the Destroyer of Dreams to accomplish his purposes and to thwart ours. You will probably recognize common predicaments and problems—lack of aptitude, impatience, procrastination, for instance. I hope you will also recognize how such common situations can be exploited by the Destroyer. I hope also to encourage you to take courage, for the Destroyer can be overcome. I have offered some suggestions to do that. For as we dare to dream, and work at realizing those dreams, God can help us build uncommonly good lives.

— 9 —

Aptitude and Attitude

It is a common practice among educational institutions to administer aptitude tests to students. These tests are designed to assess a student's ability to develop certain skills. Such information can help the teacher know what areas to emphasize with students and what to expect from them.

Aptitude is a person's natural ability to achieve something. Sometimes we may stand in awe of someone who seems able to accomplish great things with little effort. But we must guard against being intimidated into not trying something ourselves because we think we lack that aptitude. Anyone who has a natural aptitude for a certain skill should recognize it and develop it. But we should also recognize that, if we sincerely wish to accomplish a task, the attitude we bring to it can be of even greater value than having a natural aptitude.

Whereas we cannot control whether we inherit certain aptitudes, we can control our attitudes. A positive approach can compensate for what we may lack in natural ability, especially if we also recognize genuine limitations and concentrate on our best skills.

I remember a student who had a great desire to be the kicker on his high school football team. His first attempts at kicking were almost comical. He could kick the ball only a short distance, with little or no control. The ball was as likely to land out-of-bounds as on the playing field. That he had no natural aptitude for this skill was abundantly clear. What he did have, however, was an unusual determination to succeed.

He continued to practice faithfully. Long after other players had showered and gone home, he was still on the field working on his kicking. Other players steered clear of him to avoid being enlisted to return his punts as he tried again and again. He also took time to watch videos and to carefully study the techniques of successful professional players. He talked to coaches. He became acquainted with college players who kicked for their teams, and he learned from them.

His kicking improved dramatically. His efforts eventually earned him not only the position as the kicker on the high school team, but an athletic scholarship to attend his state university. He played as the kicker on the college varsity team. Later he helped train other aspiring youth in acquiring this skill.

On the other hand I vividly remember a schoolmate who had an unusual aptitude for kicking. Kicking came to him so naturally that, with very little coaching or practice, he was selected for the kicker's position on our high school team. That was as far as he went however, even though he was courted by university talent scouts. His attitude defeated him. He was not willing to pay the price of disciplined practice, so he forfeited not only a position on a team but an opportunity for a college education.

Time and time again I have watched persons with average ability achieve great things because their attitudes were right. When a task is begun with an attitude of succeeding and with enthusiasm, many obstacles can be overcome. The spirit in which we approach a task, or life in general, gives direction to our lives. Our attitudes in life might be compared to the helm of a ship which the Apostle James described: "Behold also the ships, which though they be so great, and are driven of fierce winds, yet are they turned about with a very small helm, whithersoever the governor listeth" (James 3:4).

Our attitudes govern the direction of our lives. With the correct attitudes we can raise our sights and multiply our accomplishments. We can achieve things beyond what we thought possible. For our dreams to come true we must have an attitude of trying and achieving. We have the power to choose that kind of attitude.

— 10 —

Good Dreams Only

I was deeply asleep. I had been in meetings all day and I was tired beyond belief. But the phone kept ringing. Eventually my consciousness spiraled upward through my slumber until the distant sound became real and I was awake. With sleep-filled eyes I glanced at the nearby alarm clock while I reached for the clamoring telephone. It was two o'clock in the morning. People don't generally call at two in the morning to share something pleasant. I was apprehensive. "This is Elder Allen," the voice informed me, "and we have some bad news. Two missionaries were in a car accident tonight and it looks pretty bad. It was a head-on collision. The driver of the other car was killed. The elders are in the hospital here at Shiprock. I thought you would like to know."

The sleep was gone from my eyes, and my mind was in a whirl during the few minutes it took me to check out of the motel where I was spending the night. Through the morning darkness I began driving the one-hundred-mile distance to Shiprock, New Mexico. I had learned that the accident was not the fault of the elders, but I did not yet know the extent of their injuries.

"They aren't here," said the resident physician when I arrived at the Shiprock hospital. "Considering the serious nature of their injuries, it seemed best to send them by ambulance to Farmington where the hospital is better equipped."

I continued my quest, and finally located the young elders in the Farmington hospital. The attending physicians helped me understand what I saw—concussion, broken arms and broken jaw, lacerations, and trauma. Only after receiving reassurance did I feel courageous enough to make the difficult calls to the parents of the young men.

Both elders eventually recovered and returned to missionary service. But I would here like to draw some lessons from the story of their accident.

Responsibility for the disaster was clearly established as belonging solely to the deceased driver of the other vehicle. His judgment was impaired due to extreme intoxication. The truck he was driving had crossed the road median and collided head-on into the car driven by the unsuspecting elders. The truck was instantly crushed into a misshapen hulk of twisted metal. The front of the vehicle was compressed so far that the steering wheel touched the back of the seat cushion. The other vehicle looked much the same. It too was totaled. The fact that anyone lived through the collision was an undisputed miracle.

I refer to this traumatic experience to illustrate

what happens when a law associated with our physical world is broken. This particular law is that no two things can occupy the same space at the same time. This tragedy was a dramatic illustration of what happens when this law is violated. It is a principle played out again and again in our everyday lives, one that most of us have come to understand and accept. The validity and uncompromising finality of this physical law is beyond dispute. When this law is broken unpleasant consequences can, and often do, follow. It is that simple. *"FAITH AND DOUBT CANNOT EXIST AT THE SAME TIME"*

"Is this seat taken?" Obviously no one wants to sit in a chair occupied by someone else. We brush the cat off the couch before we sit down; if we don't, an interesting scene may develop where neither party is comfortable. We take an empty bucket, not a full one, to fill with water at a well. We drive on our own side of the road if we know what's good for us, and we park only where an empty space is available. We talk about capacity crowds and about how many people a place will hold. When a movie ends, one group of patrons waits patiently for the first group to exit before they attempt to occupy the same space.

As these examples illustrate, we clearly understand and accept physical laws that govern us, and we live by them. What is not always so well understood is that there are spiritual laws just as real and just as binding.

We can apply this physical principle in a spiritual sense to our efforts to make our dreams come true. When doubt and discouragement fully occupy our minds they drive out our positive assurances just as surely as water displaces air in a jug. Good feelings flee in the presence of hate or jealousy, because those contrary feelings cannot occupy the same space at the same time.

49

Light replaces darkness. Love replaces hate or, conversely, hate replaces love. This is consistent with the teachings of the Savior and of the prophets. In the First Epistle of John we read: "He that loveth his brother abideth in the light, and there is none occasion of stumbling in him. But he that hateth his brother is in darkness, and walketh in darkness, and knoweth not whither he goeth, because that darkness hath blinded his eyes." (1 John 2:10-11.)

When the Lord told us to love our enemies (see Luke 6:27), he had our happiness in mind. Happiness is not an external condition; it is a state of the spirit, an attitude of the mind. Feelings of hate, jealousy, or contention can drive out good feelings and create an emotional imbalance that removes any chance for real happiness. That is why we cannot be contentious and spiritual at the same time. The Savior taught, "He that hath the spirit of contention is not of me, but is of the devil, who is the father of contention" (3 Nephi 11:29).

The Savior also taught us the vainness of trying to follow two masters who differ greatly in purpose: "No man can serve two masters: for either he will hate the one, and love the other; or else he will hold to the one, and despise the other. Ye cannot serve God and mammon." (Matthew 6:24.)

Another illustration might come from the Apostle Peter, who showed unusual faith. When he came down out of the ship, his faith was so great that he walked upon the water. "But when he saw the wind boisterous, he was afraid; and beginning to sink, he cried, saying, Lord, save me" (Matthew 14:30).

This is in no way intended to cast negative judgment upon Peter. He had enough faith to walk upon the water. I haven't done that lately, have you? He had tremendous faith, *until* he looked down at those boisterous waves and his faith was replaced with doubt.

Doubt crowded out faith and, with his fait
ished, he sank into the sea. "O thou of littl
the Savior said to him, "wherefore didst thou
(Matthew 14:31.)

Our doubts may sink our dreams when we allow
those doubts to replace confidence and commitment. It
would be difficult to give our best effort when feelings
of uncertainty are lurking in the shadows. The Apostle
James posed this question: "Doth a fountain send
forth at the same place sweet water and bitter? Can
the fig tree, my brethren, bear olive berries? either a
vine, figs? so can no fountain both yield salt water and
fresh." (James 3:11-12.)

So dream good dreams and don't let them be
crowded out by self-doubt or negative feelings. Choose
the good and there won't be room left for anything
else.

— 11 —

A Round
Tuit

She can be seen standing in her husband's workshop, a scroll saw in her hand, showing a determination that overshadows her inexperience. She is trying to saw a circular piece of wood out of a square of plywood. "What in the world are you making?" you might ask.

"It's for my husband," is her stern reply. "He needs this in a bad way. When I give this to him, then a lot of things we've been waiting for are going to happen. He's going to take the boys camping. He's going to fix that bottom step on the stairway and put new washers in the leaky faucet."

Picking up the round wooden object, she begins sanding off some of the rough edges and then reaches for a small pointed paintbrush. Dipping the brush into a small can of red paint, she begins scribing a label on her creation: "A Round Tuit."

"You can't believe the number of things my husband has told me we're going to do as soon as he gets a round tuit," she says grimly, "and this seems to be the only way he will get one."

Such a drama may be imaginary, but I have actually seen some "Round Tuits" on sale in novelty shops. Perhaps the need for them is more universal than we might suppose.

The other day I fixed our front doorbell. It had been performing sporadically for more than a couple of years. It would ring only when you held the button down for a sustained period of time. Even then it rang only part of the time. Determined callers could resort to knocking. But when we were all congregated in the family room at the back of our house, we could seldom hear knocking on the front door. When the doorbell didn't work, and our guests couldn't rouse us by knocking on our front door, they must have wondered about our lack of hospitality.

Finally, by some miracle, I got a round tuit. I took time to fix that doorbell. What was most disturbing to my long-suffering companion was the fact that it took me only about thirty minutes to purchase a new part for that ailing instrument and to install it. In other words we tolerated a very unpleasant situation for more than two years because I never got a round tuit. Once I even spent more than thirty minutes to make a sign to go near the erratic doorbell giving instructions on how to make it work. Sound crazy? Well, it was. But, come on now. I'll bet if you put your mind tuit you could think of times when you have done something almost as silly.

How long has it been since you wrote in your journal? Did you send that thank-you note that you had promised yourself you would? What about the new people who moved into the neighborhood? You were going to stop and wish them welcome, remember? You know, it's kind of like someone said, "Procrastination is a silly thing; it can only make me sorrow. But I can change at any time. I think I will—tomorrow!"

The foregoing examples are perhaps only little things, but the habit of procrastination can have devastating effects on the whole fiber of our lives. We seem to have a tendency to put off those things that are unpleasant or that require extra effort. "I don't have time" is a real cop-out. We all have the same number of hours in every day. How we choose to use those hours, days, and years is what makes the difference.

I remember an incident that happened some years ago when I was serving as bishop of a ward. Attendance at one of our meetings had been unpredictable and I was trying to encourage people to come more regularly.

"But, Bishop," one of my good members commented, "you need to understand that we farmers can't drop what we're doing just any time to come to a meeting."

I smiled in agreement. I had once been a farmer and I really did understand. However, I countered with this observation: "Remember last year when we were both in the elders quorum? We had a real good thing going when our softball team was part of the city league competition. I remember clearly that we seldom knew very far in advance when we would have to play. We had a great time, and if I remember correctly, you were our catcher and you never missed a single game!"

He smiled, and no further comment was needed.

The habit of procrastination may reach into our lives in much bigger ways, and opportunities with eternal consequence are lost. One person said: "Better the smallest good deed than the grandest good intention."

Overcoming our procrastinating can bring a particular satisfaction. Some individuals make a habit of attacking the unpleasant tasks first. With them out of the way, they are free to enjoy the more agreeable tasks without a nagging conscience.

We cannot assume that there will always be tomorrows. Tasks not done today may never be done. There is some validity to the proposition espoused by some, "There is no tomorrow but only today." The following poem summarizes well the ideas expressed in this chapter:

Tomorrow

He was going to be all a mortal could be—
    tomorrow.
No one would be kinder or braver than he—
    tomorrow.
A friend was troubled and weary he knew
Who'd be glad for a lift and who needed it, too.
On him he would call and see what he could do—
    tomorrow.
Each morning he'd stack up the letters he'd write—
    tomorrow.
And thought of the folks he'd fill with delight—
    tomorrow.
It was too bad, indeed, he was busy today
And hadn't a minute to stop on his way.
More time he would have to give others, he'd say—
    tomorrow.
The greatest of workers this man would have been—
    tomorrow.
The world would have known him had he ever seen
    tomorrow.

But the fact is he died, and he faded from view,
And all that he left here when living was through,
Was a mountain of things he intended to do—
    Tomorrow.

—Authorship unknown

— 12 —

Don't Lose Your Pillow

W hat on earth are you looking for?" asks one
brother. The other replies, "I'm looking for
something I lost last night. You see, during the night I
dreamed I was eating a giant marshmallow, and when
I got up this morning I couldn't find my pillow!"

In our quest for making dreams come true, we
must not lose sight of one of our most useful tools—
humor. Humor, like a pillow, can soften some of life's
hard spots. What we are doing may be very serious
and demand our best efforts, but we can impede our
progress and lessen our chances for happiness when
we take ourselves too seriously. Many awkward situations can be defused with a little appropriate humor.
When we become too anxious to succeed, we can
build tension and stress that impede our effectiveness.

Humor can provide a safety valve and help us keep our daily challenges in proper perspective. Humor can add a certain spice to life that gives it the zest that makes the difference between enjoyment and drudgery.

When my childhood friend fell into a mud puddle and began to cry, I remember how shocked I was. In my family, we had been taught that big boys don't cry; but even more important, we had been taught a much easier way to handle this sort of mishap. I had been laughed at so many times when I had a misfortune such as this that I had learned how to laugh at myself. That is not to say that we were insensitive to real injury or distress, but in the everyday type of experiences we actually found some fun when we might have found only injury.

Sometimes a simple phrase would elicit a chuckle and a vivid memory of one of our hilarious adversities. If you were to speak of a little green rope, for example, my younger brother and the rest of the family would know immediately what you had reference to. The story goes something like this: My father was making an emergency trip to town, and my brother, who was about nine or ten years old, insisted on going too. My father emphatically refused, having urgent business to transact. But as Father drove the car out of our yard, young Jerry held on to the handle of the car door and was dragged dangerously along our dirt road. Concerned for his safety, in a hurry, and in some exasperation and desperation, my father got out of the car. Jerry knew right away that he was in real trouble! Looking around for a proper instrument of education, my father spotted a short piece of rope on the edge of the road. It had been near some green paint which had spilled and hardened on its surface, making it rather stiff and hard. A few well-placed administrations of that "little green rope" onto Jerry's posterior caused him to understand clearly that he was not invited on that trip.

While it was a tough moment for him, he received little if any sympathy from the rest of the family. In fact, we thought it was really funny. Later, he too was able to see the humor of it and was heard to observe, "Dad, no one ever explained it to me quite that way before."

Naturally my father was distressed that this had taken place, but Jerry's safety was more important to him than his immediate comfort. What could have been an alienating experience became instead an addition to our list of funny occurrences. Following this incident, when Jerry required correction, it was usually sufficient to merely pose the question, "Do you want me to get that little green rope?"

So when my friend fell in the mud I expected him to laugh, not to cry. Nobody likes a crybaby. Crybabies don't even like themselves. The old saying is more than just pretty words: "Laugh, and the world laughs with you. Cry, and you cry alone."

Missionaries often face really tough situations, but they thrive on them. Guardian angels must work overtime to get them through the toughest ones, but the missionaries learn to come out smiling.

For instance, two young sister missionaries were able to see the light side of a trying experience. They were assigned to a remote mountainous area in the Arizona mission over which I presided. That area got a lot of snow and cold weather. They lived in a small trailer house. A winter cold snap had descended suddenly, and they had been forced to deal with some major hardships. It had been so cold that the water pipes in their trailer were frozen. In order to use the toilet, they had gathered snow from the ground outside, melted it on top of their propane stove, and poured the water into the toilet tank. Their only transportation was a little Chevy Luv pickup truck, but new snow, several feet deep, blocked their driveway and stranded them about thirty yards from the paved road. In order to exit, they would have to put chains on the rear wheels of the truck. Quite a task for a couple of young girls. But, don't forget, we can do almost anything if we aren't afraid to try.

They were willing to try. They had to make a trip to town because one of them had lost her contact lenses. So each attempted to fasten a chain around a wheel of the truck. They had to lie on their backs in the cold snow and, with icy fingers, stiff and nearly frozen, try to fasten the frigid, slippery chains to the wheel.

How do you put chains on a truck when you can't see what you are doing without your contact lenses? And how can you get new contacts if you don't get through the deep snow? And how do you get through the snow unless you get the chains on?

Later, as they were describing this experience to me, they were laughing and poking one another in the ribs. Do you see how a really serious situation can be helped with a little humor? By the way, they did get the chains on, they did get to town, they did get the lenses, and they lived happier ever after. They accomplished all this, and they had fun doing it.

This reminds me of two of our other sister missionaries. Their truck got stuck down in the bottom of a gulch. This is more than an inconvenience in Arizona and New Mexico. If there happens to be a rainstorm up-country, it can send a wall of water down these gulches that sweeps away everything in its path. A pickup truck would be a piece of flotsam for one of these torrents.

They were anxious, therefore, to get their truck unstuck. Finally, they decided that they would have to seek assistance. After walking several miles down a country road in a rather remote area, they came to a public telephone booth. Exercising the faith of young missionaries, a faith that is hard to duplicate, the young sisters sought the help of the Spirit. Then they opened the telephone book, selected a name, and made a call for help to a total stranger.

"Can you come and help us?" they asked. "We are six miles out of town on the dirt road leading south."

"I'll be there in a few minutes," was the reply. And the sisters weren't even surprised.

Soon the fellow showed up in a big pickup truck and, with an experienced hand, fastened a chain from his truck to the bumper of their truck, and pulled them out of the mudhole and out of the gulch. When they reached the top of the hill, the sisters got out of their truck to thank their rescuer. They learned that he had recently been contacted by the missionaries in his area and that they were teaching him the gospel. Again, they were hardly surprised. Their simple prayer of faith had been answered.

While they were talking to their rescuer, the sisters' truck, which they had left unattended, rolled back down the hill and became securely re-stuck in the same mudhole.

The sisters laughed as they related this story to me, and I chuckled with them.

Have fun with life's mudholes. We will all be stuck in some of them in one way or another.

Sunshine and Music

A laugh is just like sunshine.
It freshens all the day,

It tips the peak of life with light,
And drives the clouds away.
The soul grows glad that hears it
And feels its courage strong.
A laugh is just like sunshine
For cheering folks along.

A laugh is just like music.
It lingers in the heart,
And where its melody is heard
The ills of life depart;
And happy thoughts come crowding
Its joyful notes to greet:
A laugh is just like music
For making living sweet.

—Authorship unknown

— 13 —

Stop to Smell the Roses

My family has never seen the Grand Canyon, although we lived in Arizona for ten years and frequently made trips from Arizona to Utah. During those trips we often passed by the exit leading to this glorious site, yet we never turned off the freeway to explore. We have never seen the Grand Canyon! As you might guess, I am frequently reminded that this is the case.

I regret that we never took time to observe this wonder of nature; but, you see, we were always in a hurry to get someplace else. "We will stop next time," we said frequently, but we never did. And now we no longer live near the canyon.

Have you ever done something as foolish? Have you hurried past some lovely place? Have you noticed the roses but failed to smell them because you were in too much of a hurry to get somewhere else? On our big journey of life we are all too often in such a hurry to arrive at a particular destination that, lest we beware, we miss a lot of Grand Canyons along the way.

Dreams should not always be saved for tomorrow. In a sense tomorrow never comes anyway; there is only today. If we do not pursue our dreams today, then our dreams will never come true. How can they if they are always planned for sometime in the future? If we bypass the canyon today, if we don't smell the roses along the way, we lose that opportunity and decrease the possibilities of building the dream.

Often what we need most is not more dreams fulfilled but an appreciation for those that are already being realized. Too often, for example, we don't appreciate loved ones until they are gone. We don't value our good health until we lose it. We don't cherish freedom until some of it is lost. So much beauty surrounds us, yet we may remain oblivious to it. This was eloquently expressed by Elizabeth Barrett Browning:

> Earth's crammed with heaven,
> And every common bush afire with God;
> But only he who sees, takes off his shoes,
> The rest sit round it and pluck blackberries.

Just as we fail to see and appreciate many of God's outward creations and reverence their beauty, we may also fail to appreciate our wonderful bodies. We may look with envy upon those who seem to be more fortunate. But one sensitive author reminds us to look more thoughtfully:

The World Is Mine

Today upon a bus,
I saw a lovely maid with golden hair;
I envied her—she seemed so gay—
And I wished I were as fair.
When suddenly she rose to leave,
I saw her hobble down the aisle;
She had one foot and wore a crutch,
But as she passed, a smile;
Oh, God, forgive me when I whine;
I have two feet—the world is mine!

And then I stopped to buy some sweets.
The lad who sold them had such charm.
I talked with him—he said to me:
"It's nice to talk with folks like you.
"You see," he said, "I'm blind."
Oh, God, forgive me when I whine;
I have two eyes—the world is mine!

Then walking down the street,
I saw a child with eyes of blue.
He stood and watched the others play;
It seemed he knew not what to do.
I stopped for a moment, then I said:
"Why don't you join the others, dear?"
He looked ahead without a word,
And then I knew, he could not hear.
Oh, God, forgive me when I whine;
I have two ears—the world is mine!

With feet to take me where I'd go,
With eyes to see the sunset's glow,
With ears to hear what I would know,
Oh, God, forgive me when I whine;
I'm blessed indeed! The world is mine.

—Authorship unknown

When someone *doesn't* see the beauty, he is no better off than one who *can't* see it. We can be blind even when we can see, as expressed by Harry Kemp in a poem entitled "Blind":

> The Spring blew trumpets of color;
> Her green sang in my brain.
> I heard a blind man groping
> Tap-tap-tap with his cane.
>
> I pitied him in his blindness;
> But can I boast, "I see"?
> Perhaps there walks a spirit
> Close by, who pities me.
>
> A spirit who hears me tapping
> The five-sensed cane of mind
> Amid such unguessed glories
> That I am worse than blind.

We should not limit our appreciation to big things. Life is packed with many small "unguessed glories." The habit of being grateful and enjoying daily pleasures is what we need to strive for.

While presiding over a mission of the Church, I received a rather touching letter, part of which I share with you. This missionary wrote:

> I wasn't accustomed to believing that things were good. Since I have been on my mission, I have started seeing the good in a lot of things—the warm sunlight in my room, the cool breeze and the fresh pine scent from the forest after a gentle rain, purring kittens, little lambs and goats, children giggling in pure delight and fun. I have started seeing the good in people and my soul has begun to ache with a desire to serve them and to lift them

with the gospel message. I have discovered that there really is joy in giving, especially when I have helped make someone else happy. This has brought me joy.

The Lord has promised that when we receive with gratitude that with which he blesses us, he will bless us further: "And he who receiveth all things with thankfulness shall be made glorious; and the things of this earth shall be added unto him, even an hundred fold, yea, more" (D&C 78:19).

Serious and frequent reflection upon the good things that surround us helps sharpen our awareness and strengthen our appreciation. One of the best ways to feel and give expression to our appreciation is through daily thanksgiving to our Father in Heaven. As we pause each day to thank him, we can focus upon the many beautiful things and favorable circumstances that surround us. We begin to have eyes that see more clearly and ears that hear with greater understanding.

My two young children taught me a lesson in gratitude. We were traveling in our automobile through a remote area of Wyoming, returning to our home in Utah. Some dark black clouds were rapidly forming in the west, churning in fearsome billows, and coming rapidly toward us. I had lived in Wyoming for many years, and I knew that being caught in a heavy storm in this territory might be dangerous. But I was undecided on the best course of action. Should I try to drive faster to get ahead of the worst of the threatening storm, or should I stop along the side of the road and try to weather it?

But the choices were quickly gone. The force of that wind-driven summer hailstorm engulfed us. Hailstones were driven with such ferocity that the ice, usually round, was distorted into jagged, oblong pieces. They pounded frighteningly on our car with a sound like the smash of a heavy sledgehammer. The first stones shattered out windshield in a half dozen places, making huge asterisk-like patterns. We had no choice but to stop. As the pounding continued I worried that the windows might shatter completely and let the storm in upon us.

Then I heard a small voice from the back seat. "Daddy, why don't we say a prayer?" I offered a simple prayer. The storm passed beyond us, leaving us quickly as it had appeared.

We resumed our journey, hampered by the cracked windshield. After driving quietly for a few miles, a soft voice spoke again from the back seat. "Daddy, don't you think we should say thanks?" We pulled to the side of the road—this time because we wanted to—and offered a prayer of sincere gratitude.

Let us not be like the sailor whose ship was resting in fresh water while he suffered with thirst, not realizing that his dream of pure water was all about him. Our dreams come true every day as we open our eyes and our hearts to the good things around us. As we do, let us follow the admonition of the prophet Amulek: "Live in thanksgiving daily, for the many mercies and blessings which he doth bestow upon you" (Alma 34:38).

— 14 —

Be
Square

A friend of mine built a barn. If I had explained the principle of 6x8x10 I could have saved him a lot of grief. His building was not square and so, as he proceeded with the construction, the problem of being out of square, and therefore not fitting just right, kept reappearing over and over with each succeeding step of construction. Experienced builders understand clearly the importance of this principle. They continually use tools like a framing square, a level, a plumb bob, a stretched string, and a transit to be certain a building is true. The principle of 6x8x10, simply put, is to determine as nearly as possible the proposed right angle. Measuring six feet from the corner in one direction and eight feet in the other will result in a diagonal of ten feet. When this is achieved the angle is square.

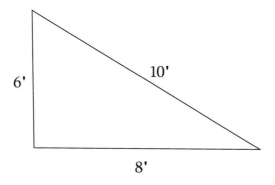

Being crooked has a generally negative connotation and creates problems in building construction. But even greater problems appear when this is applied to the lives of individuals.

For example, who would ever consider trusting a person labeled as crooked? I don't suppose we would appreciate being called a crook either. What is a crook anyway? A crook is someone who isn't straight. Well then, what does it mean to be straight? Some of the first words that come to mind are honest, trustworthy, dependable, genuine, upright, honorable, fair.

The term *straight* might be used to describe an undeviating course of action or commitment. People who have abandoned bad behavior patterns are said to have "gone straight." Generally we consider a person who is straight to be the kind of person who can be counted on. Someone correctly observed that "a straight line is the shortest distance in morals as well as in geometry."

What does all this have to do with making dreams come true? If we want our lives to be happy, they must be on the square. Anything less than this will eventually result in unhappiness and sorrow and the problem will continue to multiply in many facets of our lives until it is corrected. Our compass for life should point us in an unfaltering course, not a crooked path. Perhaps the reason there are so many crooked paths is that men, like streams of water, often follow the path of least resistance.

We would do well to follow the example of the Lord, who clearly understands eternal purposes. According to his word: "God doth not walk in crooked paths, neither doth he turn to the right hand nor to the left, neither doth he vary from that which he hath said, therefore his paths are straight, and his course is one eternal round" (D&C 3:2).

One morning a teacher brought a simple framing square to her classroom. This unusual teaching tool captured everyone's attention. "This is a square," she announced. Hearing those words, the students turned in concert to look at Craig. He blushed with embarrassment. Apparently he had earned the title of being "a square," someone the others considered dull and rigid. He was a good student, of conservative tastes, who had shown unusual courage and commitment to maintain his personal ideals. He was unbending in the face of severe peer-group pressure, and so was given the label.

The teacher ignored the students' first reaction and went on to explain the purpose and importance of a square. Then she explained the relationship between keeping buildings square and of people being square. She skillfully extracted from her young students how essential it is in our society to have standards by which things can be measured. She even brought several homemade rulers which were of different lengths because they were inaccurately marked. "Which one of them is right?" she challenged them. She then explained the role of the Bureau of Standards and the essential function this institution performs in providing standardization, stability, and order in our society.

As the end of the class period drew near, the teacher gave the students the opportunity to express themselves. With some effort to control his pent-up emotions, Craig rose to his feet, looked at each of his classmates, and said with strong conviction, "For the first time in my life I feel proud to be called a square."

The squares of this world provide the anchors of society; because of them, justice can prevail. Truth in its purity is the foundation of character. It requires courage to live our lives in harmony with our ideals. To be a square is not always the easiest course, but lasting dreams are only fulfilled as we exercise this kind of courage.

To use dishonest practices in order to realize a dream might be compared to using crooked structures in a building. Sooner or later, the fault will reappear, the dream will become a nightmare.

The man who makes money or acquires fame dishonestly is proclaiming that he esteems these above his personal honor, and without that honor, he will ultimately fall. The continuing prosperity of an individual, a city, or a nation ultimately comes to rest on its integrity. This integrity is shown by promises kept, by confidences honored, by honest communications, by our own personal conduct being consistent with our verbal commitments.

For dreams to come true we must sometimes wait, secure in the knowledge that truth will ultimately triumph. No lasting success or happiness can come that is not founded upon truth.

So as we dream our dreams, let us build squarely. Apply the six, the eight, and see if we get ten. Then our fondest dreams will ultimately come true.

— 15 —

Hang In There

The intended message of this chapter is effectively expressed in this verse entitled, "Perseverance":

> The ninety and nine are with dreams content;
> But the hope of a world made new
> Is the hundredth man who is grimly bent
> On making that dream come true.
>
> —Authorship unknown

I recall an experience from some years ago when someone who was searching for me finally found me. "There is a long-distance telephone call for you," I was informed. "They have been trying hard to reach you all day." When I heard this I imagined all sorts of dire things that might have gone wrong. In my capacity as an agriculture teacher, I was at the Midland Empire Fair in Billings, Montana, with a group of my students who were exhibiting livestock. It was difficult to reach any of us, since we were roughing it by sleeping outside in our sleeping bags in order to be close to our livestock, who required our constant vigilance.

I soon learned that my imagined fears were unfounded. This call turned out to be one of those "good news calls." The caller was a representative from a national arc welding company that sponsored a nationwide welding contest each year. He was calling to ask me to have some pictures taken. The picture was to be of me and my students posed with the projects they had completed. The company asked us to have a professional photographer take the photos and to send them the bill. The results of this contest were not to be announced until the next month. I surmised that we were not in last place if they wanted our picture taken. The suspense was almost too much for us to bear.

Imagine our thrill to learn later that we had won first and third place in this nationwide contest. Our picture appeared in national magazines, brochures, and newspapers. It was pretty heady excitement, and the boys each won an attractive amount of prize money as well as great personal satisfaction.

Our fun was dampened slightly when another student approached the boy who had won first place and asked him to share his winnings with him. I was brought in to help arbitrate the situation.

The project had begun as a joint venture between the two boys. They were building from scratch a tandem-wheeled, tilting-framed, flatbed machinery trailer. It was an ambitious project for high school students with limited time in shop class. It required many skills and much hard work.

As the year progressed it appeared that the project would never be finished. Their dream of completing this beautiful trailer and of winning a national prize grew dim. The boys reacted in different ways, however. One of them took the easy way out and simply quit. His partner took another approach and began working harder and longer. He spent his noon hours and free time before and after school cutting, welding, drilling, grinding, and painting. He put on the afterburners and completed the project and the application forms just before the school year ended. We would have to wait until the beginning of the next school year for a panel of judges to rate the entries and announce the results of the competition.

That student who won the competition—first place in the whole United States—generously shared some of his winnings with the boy who had briefly helped him. But the greater victory was really his. He had stuck it out. Without his perseverance there would have been no prize money, no national recognition, no dream come true. The boy who dropped out was puzzled when I told him: "You had better go home and read the story of 'The Little Red Hen.'"

It was David Lloyd George who said, "There is nothing so fatal to character as half-finished tasks." Realizing dreams requires, most of all, determination and perseverance. Many ambitious endeavors are abandoned at the most critical moment when, with a little more effort, a little more patience, success could have been reached.

I worked with a group of young boys a number of years ago to construct a block building. We spent considerable time laying out the dimensions, excavating for the footings, constructing forms for the cement, and pouring the cement. Then we leveled the area with appropriate backfill.

After the floor area was leveled, we had to go back and excavate trenches for the water and sewer lines. After installing the plumbing, we backfilled again and prepared to pour the cement floor. We had worked very hard for some time but, to the casual observer, we had accomplished very little. There was only a simple pad of cement showing a few inches above the ground. When we started putting up the walls however, it seemed like we built the whole structure in a few days. It now stood tall and erect for all to see.

The strong but essential foundations for great structures are often not visible. This is true whether the task is gaining an education for a future career, gaining skills and experience, or getting a business started. These foundations require a great effort and are essential. Defeat in completing tasks usually comes when a builder loses sight of his dream and, failing to see visible results, becomes discouraged and quits, often when victory is almost in sight.

We live in an age of fast foods, fast cars, fast service. We are often too impatient to order from a catalog because we want things right now! This makes it even more important for us to remember that some things, often the best things, require time. We cannot turn up the incubator to make our chickens hatch faster. With fast-track careers, as with over-incubated eggs, we may have scrambled eggs, scrambled careers, and scrambled dreams.

Don L. Lind, who became an astronaut for NASA, discussed the necessity of persistence:

> After some of the Apollo delays and setbacks, critics of the program wanted us to quit—it was too hard and required too much of our national effort.

I recall that when I was learning to play the piano and when I was learning German and calculus, it was easy to get discouraged. Progress seemed so slow, and I was not sure I was getting anyplace. It took three and a half years of applying to NASA before they would accept my application for the astronaut program. I was told "no" officially, formally, and finally, over a dozen times. I suppose I am just stubborn, but each time there was another chance, I would try again. In the mean time, of course, I kept up the physical fitness program, and the flying and the studying.

Finally, all the effort paid off–I received a call from "Deke" Slayton inviting me to join the space program as an astronaut. The goal had been achieved! ("'The Eagle Has Landed!'" *Instructor,* October 1970, p. 361.)

President Ezra Taft Benson counseled, "To press on in noble endeavors, even while surrounded by a cloud of depression, will eventually bring you out on top into the sunshine" ("Do Not Despair," *Ensign,* November 1974, p. 67).

A poem was penned many years ago by Edgar A. Guest that helps us understand the importance of hanging on:

The Quitter

Fate handed the quitter a bump and he dropped–
The road seemed too rough to go, so he stopped;
He thought of his hurt, and there came to his mind
The easier path he was leaving behind;
"Oh, it's all much too hard," said the quitter right
    then;
"I'll stop where I am and not try it again."

He sat by the road and he made up his tale
To tell when men asked why he happened to fail.
A thousand excuses flew up to his tongue,
And these on the thread of his story he strung.
But the truth of the matter he didn't admit—
He never once said, "I was frightened and quit."
Whenever the quitter sits down by the road
And drops from the struggle to lighten his load,
He can always recall to his own peace of mind
A string of excuses for falling behind;
But somehow or other, he can't think of one
Good reason for battling and going right on.
Oh, when the bump comes and fate hands you a
   jar,
Don't baby yourself, boy, whoever you are,
Don't pity yourself and talk over your woes,
Don't think up excuses for dodging the blows,
But stick to the battle and see the thing through,
And don't be a quitter, whatever you do.

When I participated on our high school track team, we had a brilliant coach. On some of the distance runs, like the half-mile run, he would put a runner in to step up the pace. We never knew who it was going to be. This runner would sprint as fast as he could go, with no intention of finishing. At some point in the race he would drop out. Some runners, especially those who had not learned to pace themselves, would run fast to keep up with him and then run out of steam before crossing the finish line. Our coach had trained us to not worry about these competitors. What counted was not who started out like a streak of lightening, but who crossed the finish line first. That is not to say that a fast start is not desired, but it is more important to keep a pace that can be sustained until the race is over. The man farthest ahead accomplishes nothing unless he crosses the line.

Growing up on the farm, I learned early that it was not how many acres we planted that counted, it was how many acres we harvested.

It takes grit to be a finisher, a winner. As one author put it, "A quitter never wins and a winner never quits."

President Calvin Coolidge said it this way: "Nothing in the world can take the place of persistency. . . . Talent will not; nothing is more common than unsuccessful men with talent. Genius will not; unrewarded genius is a proverb. Education will not; the world is full of educated derelicts. Persistence and determination alone are omnipotent."

— 16 —

Green Watermelon

It had been a lovely summer. An early spring had melted the snow and replaced barren limbs with green leafy branches. The late frost had missed us this year, and the garden appeared to be the best we had ever grown. It even looked like we would have watermelon, an uncommon occurrence because of our short growing season. We watched the young melon vines develop with their peculiar-looking leaves, and everyone was excited when blossoms began to appear. We watered and weeded the plants faithfully and took pride when blossoms turned to little green cylinders with the promise of becoming larger. Their growth seemed painfully slow, and we wondered if the melons would ever be big enough to make us smile when we broke them open to taste the sweet fruit and to spit out black seeds on the ground.

After what seemed an eternity to our young minds, the melons became large. We now began to wonder when the inside would change from green to red. Imagine our dismay when one young and impatient family member, wielding a large butcher knife, cut a big plug from every single large melon in the patch to determine which were ripe. All were green and immature, of course, but now they were also ruined.

The farm helped us in many ways to develop patience. Through painful experiences, we learned to accept nature's timetable. We learned that eggs take a given time to incubate. We watched hopefully for the new little chicks to hatch and came to know that some good things take time and patience.

One of our favorite activities was making homemade root beer. Our root beer became better with time, but because we were impatient, the root beer was often just approaching its prime as we drank the last bottle. Too often we came in from the garden with a new ear of corn before the kernels were fully developed or with a tomato not quite red that should have spent a few more days on the vine.

Today we live in a fast-moving society. We are often caught up in a frenzy of wanting everything right now. We don't want to wait. Fast food establishments do a thriving business not always because of the quality of their product but because they offer the convenience of not waiting. Ring a bell, and your order will be ready almost instantly. "Buy now," many merchants advise, "and pay later. Buy from us, and we will give you instant home delivery."

Such conveniences may make it difficult for us to develop the essential quality of patience. There are many hazards connected with impatience. Impatience can lead to frustration and discouragement when things don't happen when we want them to.

Persevering through the long years of preparation for an occupation requires patience and resolve. We must patiently deny ourselves now for rewards that will come later. We learn some skills only through repetition and maturity.

In pursuing our dreams, we must guard against expecting and wanting too much too soon. There are some roads that have no shortcuts. In those cases shortcuts turn out to be the long way around and may lead us to a different and poorer, compromised destination. The essence of this thought was wonderfully expressed by Stephen Crane in his poem called "Other Roads":

> The wayfarer,
> Perceiving the pathway to truth,
> Was struck with astonishment.
> It was thickly grown with weeds.
> "Ha," he said,
> "I see that none has passed here
> In a long time."
> Later he saw that each weed
> Was a singular knife.
> "Well," he mumbled at last,
> "Doubtless there are other roads."

There will be other roads when we are not willing to pay the full price, but that is not how dreams are fulfilled. Downhill roads are easier to follow; there are fewer demands and more time left in which to play. But it is the upward path, patiently traveled, that gets us there.

We may also show our impatience by attempting to

acquire all the material things we think we must have now. This can put us on a roller coaster of borrowing and paying for things twice over. Moneylenders thrive on the high interest rates they can command because of our impatience.

Our impatience may generate dissatisfaction with our employment. We want to be foreman today and chief director tomorrow. Experience, which takes time, may be our only teacher, a teacher who serves best when we are patient.

Sometimes we meet with severe adversity and discouragement. Our dreams may seem far away. Life is unfair! Why me? As difficult as these times are, they may be the best opportunities for developing the quality of patience. The Apostle Paul, writing to the Romans, said, "We glory in tribulations . . . : knowing that tribulation worketh patience; and patience, experience; and experience, hope" (Romans 5:3-4).

So give your melons time to bask and mature in the noonday sun. Wait until they are ready, then call all your friends around and slice thick, sweet, red slices and have an old-fashioned melon bust! Your dream has come true.

— 17 —

Stand Up and Be Counted

If you are to make your dreams come true, you must have courage.

I have in my file a picture of a young man lying dead on the highway near his demolished automobile. The caption beneath the picture reads simply, "Portrait of a Dead Chicken." The tragic scene graphically illustrates the twisted concept of what courage really is. This young man, playing a game of "chicken," feared the disapproval and non-acceptance of his peers more than he feared death.

There has probably never been a time in history when personal moral courage is needed more than it is today. In a world filled with a myriad of choices there are more and more negative alternatives offered to us. Making right choices often requires moral courage of the highest order and is not always the popular thing to do. One runs the risk of unpopularity or even ridicule. Physical courage is a priceless possession, but even more to be prized is the acquisition of moral courage and integrity.

Courage does not necessarily mean the absence of fear. It means, rather, possessing the internal strength and integrity necessary to do the right thing in spite of fears. It means doing not what is easy but what is good.

We are not being courageous when our fear of the unknown, the fear of trying something new, prevents us from exploring new horizons. Too often we become victims of complacency. We settle into a pattern of comfort and do not exercise the courage required to change our circumstances, our ideas, our locations, our occupations, our dreams. It is easier and far less threatening to drift, unresisting, with the current, and to lose ourselves in unchallenged conformity.

To act upon new, fresh, unexplored ideas in the face of risking failure or ridicule is courageous. Too many dreams are unfulfilled or never begun because they are stifled by the fear of not succeeding. Better to dare and fail than to fear to try.

Another form of courage is shown when we are not afraid to cry, to laugh, or to show our real feelings. A courageous person is not afraid to show true emotion. In an age of pseudo-sophistication, an increasing number of people mask their feelings because they perceive that showing emotion is incompatible with the macho image they want to project. Much is lost therefore that could bring joy into the lives of others. There would be a greater sensitivity, a deeper appreciation for delicate feelings, and an extension of love and sympathy that might otherwise be lost, if we dared to risk appearing maudlin or emotional.

Courage does not require emotional sterility. War heroes who have courageously faced danger show another kind of courage when they are not ashamed to shed tears as they greet loved ones or when they see their national colors parade past them.

Elder Gordon B. Hinckley referred to moral courage when he related an experience he had with a courageous young man who had served in the military: "I talked with another young man . . . recently returned from the war. He too had walked the jungle patrols, his heart pounding with fear. But reluctantly he admitted that the greatest fear he had was the fear of ridicule. The men of his company laughed at him, taunted him, plastered him with a nickname that troubled him." This brave young man, however, rose above the jeers of his companions and thus showed a different kind of bravery. (See Gordon B. Hinckley, "'Rise, and Stand Upon Thy Feet,'" *Improvement Era,* December 1968, pp. 69-70.) It is difficult to explain or even to understand, but this kind of courage is often harder to acquire than facing enemy gunfire.

Courage grows in doing small, everyday things correctly, in standing firm on matters of personal standards and convictions. With the daily exercise of small but correct choices, courage can take root and grow strong, thus preparing us for greater storms of testing when they come.

There is a time to be firm in defending what we know is right, a time to stand up and be counted. We thrill when we read of Brigham Young leading a company of pioneers on their journey to the Salt Lake Valley. Plagued with all kinds of adversity, physical hardships, and discouragement, some would have turned back from their dream. But the courageous leader hitched his team of horses to the wagon and started down the trail, without looking back. The fearful

Saints, catching the spirit of Brigham's commitment, took courage from him and followed.

Where moral courage and commitment are concerned, one must remember the Old Testament prophet, Joshua. In his exhortations to the faltering children of Israel, he admonished them: "Be ye therefore very courageous to keep and do all that is written in the book of the law of Moses, that ye turn not aside therefrom to the right hand or to the left" (Joshua 23:6). Then, after giving them further instruction, he gave the challenge that has rung down through the ages: "Choose you this day whom ye will serve; . . . but as for me and my house, we will serve the Lord" (Joshua 24:15).

This kind of courage, to stand firm and sometimes alone, is just as important today. There is a time to be counted. There is a time to say: "This is what I believe. This is what I will do, and this is what I will not do. This is what I stand for. You do what you will, but as for me and my house . . . "

Dreams can come true when we are honest with ourselves and possess the courage and commitment to stick to our standards and convictions. This will inspire self-confidence and give birth to the inner peace and tranquility that come from a clear conscience.

Courage is within reach of us all when we understand that we are never alone. It is as the Apostle Paul expressed to his beloved companion Timothy: "For God hath not given us the spirit of fear; but of power, and of love, and of a sound mind" (2 Timothy 1:7). We have no need to fear when we are honest and when we are straight with the Lord. When he is with us, what should we fear?

— 18 —

Keep Rolling

Pure spring water splashing and sparkling down the mountainside is beautiful to behold. It is a precious treasure, bringing with it a bouquet of life and vitality. Its course can be traced by the verdant growth surrounding its banks and sustained by its presence.

When this water reaches its destination it must find some new course to follow. If it merely accumulates, going nowhere, simply resting; it soon loses its freshness and grows stagnant. With passive existence as its only purpose, moss begins to grow, choking and strangling it. Active fish swim away in search of fresher waters.

Thus it is with us in the stream of life. Unless our current of activity keeps moving, continually giving, exploring, receiving; our lives may grow sluggish and finally stagnate. The stimulating freshness and vitality is lost when we have no purpose or continued growth.

Life is a continuing process. There is no holding pattern. We are either progressing or regressing. Muscles unused grow flabby. Gardens untended grow weedy. Friendships unsustained grow weaker. Tools unused become dull and covered with rust. Skills unpracticed are diminished. Hair uncombed becomes unruly. Houses left empty soon deteriorate, take on a different appearance, and begin to look run-down. And so it goes in every walk of life. A dream once realized must be sustained just as a fire once kindled needs to be constantly replenished; otherwise the flame will flicker, grow dim, and die.

In a similar comparison, living plants need to continue to grow. One of the most certain ways to determine the vitality of a living plant is to check the rate of new and vigorous growth. When no new growth is evident it is generally an indication that the plant is in a state of dormancy or remission. If it is to continue to live, a tree must add a new growth ring, no matter how small, every year.

So it is with our lives. Dreams fulfilled cannot be sustained without continued efforts or they will fade, grow dim, and diminish.

When our lives are filled with purpose, we are able to greet each day enthusiastically, seeing each day as a fresh page awaiting our writing. It has been said that the biggest room in the world is the room for improvement. This quest alone should keep our stream fresh as we conquer fears, develop new talents, acquire new knowledge. There are people to meet we have never met. There are places to see we have never seen. There are books we have never read.

Not all dreams need to be centered upon self.

Plateaus reached may provide a new foundation as we reach out and extend ourselves to help others. Some of life's greatest rewards and pleasures come from watching others achieve, knowing that we have contributed in some small way to their success. Dreams shared are sweeter dreams than dreams we dream alone.

So keep your life filled with purpose. Let your path be marked by deeds that sustain life, that blossom into works that bear fruit and bless all those who come near.

Climb On

Dare to dream,
To climb steep mountains
Of desire,
Though slopes are rough,
And boulders strewn
Along the way.

By that first step,
Begin
To make that dream
Come true.
Born of desire,
Fed by courage.

Not in sudden flight,
But by small steps
Move closer,
Each step nearer.
So far away,
Climb on.

Wipe away the tears
And smile.
Patch bruised knees.
Climb on

To better dreams
You dared not dream.

Say thanks
Along the way, and then
Climb on.
Wipe the sweated brow,
Breathe deeply; then
Plod on.

Up the straight path,
The only way.
Pay the price,
And rise with toil
To where the air
Is fresh and clean.

This mountain,
Does it crest?
Where does it end?
The bright clouds billow
Near your head.
The air is thin,
Legs are weary.

The top, you say,
Is only
As high as one dare dream.
Now you see
That all the best
Of dreams are yet to be.
So dare to dream!

—Wayne B. Lynn

About the Author

Wayne B. Lynn was born and raised in Powell, Wyoming, and received his B.S. degree from the University of Wyoming. He began his association with the Church Educational System as a seminary teacher in 1956, and has since served that organization in several capacities, including seminary coordinator for southern Arizona and director of seminary special curriculum. He accepted the assignment to become director of Church Curriculum Planning and Development in 1973, and has since served as director of Church magazines and as the assistant managing director for Church Curriculum Planning/Programs. He is presently advisor to Church Curriculum Planning and Development.

The author has published numerous articles in Church magazines and other publications. He is co-author of the book *Tom Trails: A New Beginning* and is author of the book *Lessons from Life*.

The author and his wife, the former Roita Monk, have eleven children. The family resides in Centerville, Utah.